Hello! My name is Arty. I'm the troll in that famous story about the goats. You know, the one with all the trip-trapping across a bridge.

Are you surprised to see me? Did you think I was done for when the biggest goat kicked me off the bridge?

Here, have some homemade bread and jam. (It's wild strawberry.)
Settle back, and I'll tell you the REAL story.

3

I've never been like other trolls.

In Troll School, I got good grades – which meant I was the worst in my class. (Trolls aren't supposed to be clever.) Instead of practising roars and chest-thumping, I made art and baked pies.

I wasn't big and clumsy. I didn't even smell bad!

"Are you sure you're a troll?" the other pupils teased. "Maybe you're an elf!"

When we finished school, the Troll Placement Board gave us jobs. I was to guard a little bridge in the middle of nowhere. The other trolls laughed. But to me, the job was perfect.

Listen, MY BRIDGE IS SO COOL!

The Story of THE THREE BILLY GOATS GRUFF

as Told by THE TROLL

by Nancy Loewen

illustrated by Cristian Bernardini

raintree

a Capstone company — publishers for children

Raintree is an imprint of Capstone Global Library Limited, a company
incorporated in England and Wales having its registered office at
264 Banbury Road, Oxford, OX2 7DY – Registered company number: 6695582

www.raintree.co.uk
myorders@raintree.co.uk

Editor: Jill Kalz
Designer: Lori Bye
Premedia Specialist: Tori Abraham

Original illustrations © Capstone Global Library Limited 2018
Originated by Capstone Global Library Limited

ISBN 978 1 4747 5344 9
22 21 20 19 18
10 9 8 7 6 5 4 3 2 1

British Library Cataloguing in Publication Data
A full catalogue record for this book is available from the British Library.

All the internet addresses (URLs) given in this book were valid at the time
of going to press. However, due to the dynamic nature of the internet, some
addresses may have changed, or sites may have changed or ceased to exist
since publication. While the author and publisher regret any inconvenience
this may cause readers, no responsibility for any such changes can be
accepted by either the author or the publisher.

Printed and bound in the United Kingdom.

I loved my bridge! In my cozy home, I wrote poetry, danced and cooked. I even played my flute.

Once in a while I saw three goats in the distance. But as soon as they saw me looking at them, the biggest goat ran away. The other two followed him.

One day a crow dropped a letter on my head.

Deer Dear Deer Arty,
UR giving trolls a good name,
witch is very vary BAD. Get meen meen, or we will remove U from
UR post.
       THE TROLL PATROL

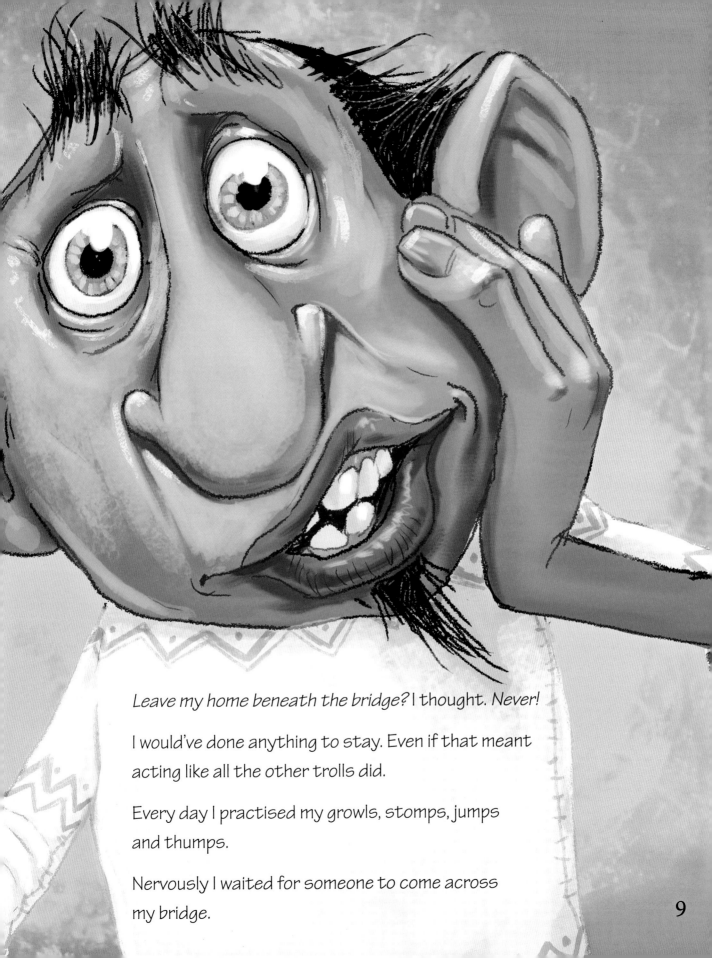

Leave my home beneath the bridge? I thought. *Never!*

I would've done anything to stay. Even if that meant acting like all the other trolls did.

Every day I practised my growls, stomps, jumps and thumps.

Nervously I waited for someone to come across my bridge.

9

Finally, my chance came. It was a beautiful summer's day. I was just about to make a pot of my world-class fish stew when I heard a clicking overhead.

TRIP-TRAP, TRIP-TRAP

This was it!

I hopped on top of the bridge and said, "WHO'S TRIPPING ACROSS MY BRIDGE?"

A little goat looked at me curiously. "*You're* the troll?" he said. "Hmm. OK."

"Yes!" I yelled. "And I'm going to GOBBLE YOU UP!"

"Oh, you don't want to eat *me*," the little goat said. "Wait for my brother. He's much bigger. He'll come along soon."

"Fine!" I said, and the goat trotted off with a grin.

11

Back beneath the bridge, I calmed myself with a few sips of pine
needle tea. Pretty soon I heard **TRIP-TRAP, TRIP-TRAP.**

I scrambled onto the bridge and tried again.
"WHO'S TRIPPING ACROSS MY BRIDGE?" I yelled.

This goat was bigger than the first. He didn't seem scared either.
"Oh, hey!" he said. "We just want to graze in that amazing patch
of grass over there. Are you cool with that?"

"Sure, that's–," I started to say, then caught myself. "I mean,
I'M GOING TO GOBBLE YOU UP!"

"Um, maybe you could wait for my big brother?" the goat said.
"He's huge."

"Fine!" I waved the goat off.

13

Before I could refresh my tea . . .

TRIP-TRAP! TRIP-TRAP!

For the third time I pulled myself onto the bridge.

"WHO'S THAT TRAMPING ACROSS MY BRIDGE?"

I said to the biggest goat I'd ever seen. I thumped my chest. "I'm going to **GOBBLE YOU UP** . . . like, **RIGHT NOW!** . . . Yep, that's exactly what I'm going to do! Gobble. You. **UP!** Just watch me!"

The big goat stood in front of me, trembling.

"Wait a minute," I said. "Are you really scared?"

He nodded.

"Me too," I confessed in a rush. "I don't want to hurt anyone, really. But the Troll Patrol says I have to either act like a troll or move. And I really love my bridge."

The goat continued to stare at me. "I might be big," he whispered, "but I'm not brave."

"Do your brothers tease you?" I asked.

"Sometimes," he admitted.

"They didn't think you would actually come to the bridge, did they?" I said.

He shook his head.

"But you DID," I told him. "You were scared, and you came here anyway. So you really ARE brave."

"I am?" he asked.

"Yes!" I said.

Oh, this couldn't have worked out better.

"Let's give them all a good show," I said. "We'll just *pretend* to fight. Your brothers will change their minds about you. And the Troll Patrol will change its mind about me!"

And that's just what we did.

These days, my life under the bridge is better than ever. Every so often, Big Bad Billy and I put on a huge pretend fight. It's making him feel better about himself. My troll skills must be improving too. I haven't received any more letters from the Troll Patrol.

Now, how about some more bread and jam?

Think about it

Describe how Arty is different from other trolls. Use the illustrations in the book to support your answer.

What were your thoughts when you saw the biggest goat for the first time? How did you expect him to act? How was the character different from what you expected?

This story is told from the point of view of the troll. If the biggest goat were telling this story, what details would change?

Look online to find a traditional telling of "The Three Billy Goats Gruff" story. How is this version of the story the same? How is it different?

Glossary

character person, animal or creature in a story
point of view way of looking at something
version account of something from a certain point of view

Find out more

Books

Rudyard Kipling's Just So Stories, retold by Elli Woollard
(Macmillan Children's Books, 2017)

The Orchard Book Of Aesop's Fables, Michael Morpurgo
(Orchard Books, 2014)

Website

www.bbc.co.uk/programmes/b03g64r9
You can listen to other stories featuring talking animals –
Aesop's Fables – on this website.

Look for all the books in the series:

Believe Me, Goldilocks Rocks!
Believe Me, I Never Felt a Pea!
For Real, I Paraded in My Underpants!
Frankly, I'd Rather Spin Myself a New Name!
Frankly, I Never Wanted to Kiss Anybody!
Honestly, Our Music Stole the Show!
Honestly, Red Riding Hood Was Rotten!
Listen, My Bridge Is SO Cool!
No Kidding, Mermaids Are a Joke!

No Lie, I Acted Like a Beast!
No Lie, Pigs (and Their Houses) CAN Fly!
Really, Rapunzel Needed a Haircut!
Seriously, Cinderella Is SO Annoying!
Seriously, Snow White Was SO Forgetful!
Truly, We Both Loved Beauty Dearly!
Trust Me, Hansel and Gretel Are SWEET!
Trust Me, Jack's Beanstalk Stinks!
Truthfully, Something Smelled Fishy!